NEW RED BIKE!

James E. Ransome

I Like to Read®

HOLIDAY HOUSE • NEW YORK

Tom rides his new bike
with both hands
on the handlebars
and with his helmet on.

Tom rides up

and down

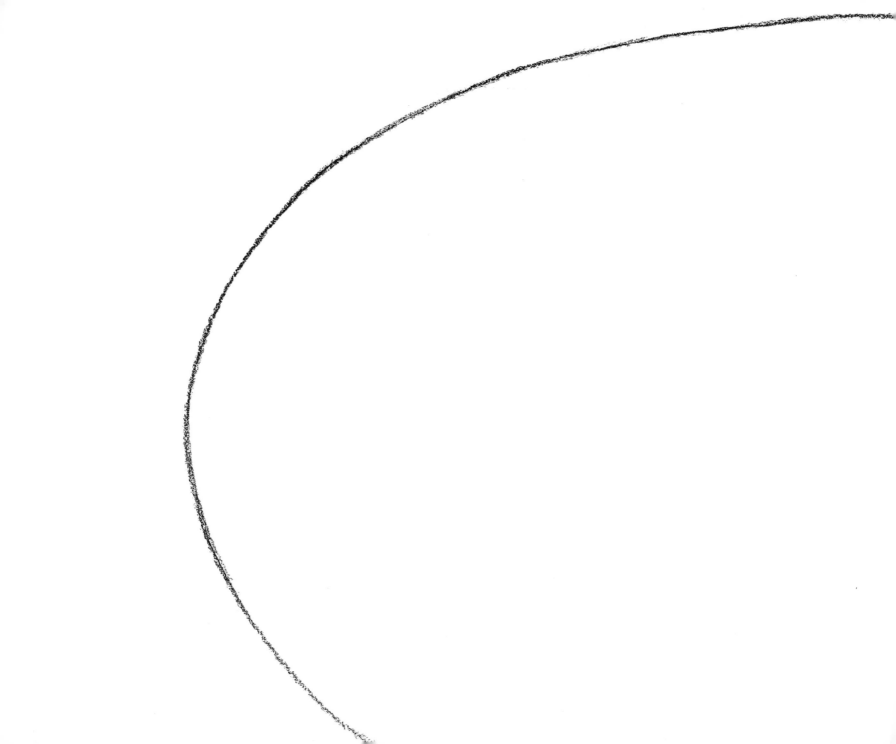

and around in circles.

He zooms down the hill,

around
the curve,

and back up.

Then he sweeps down to Sam's house.

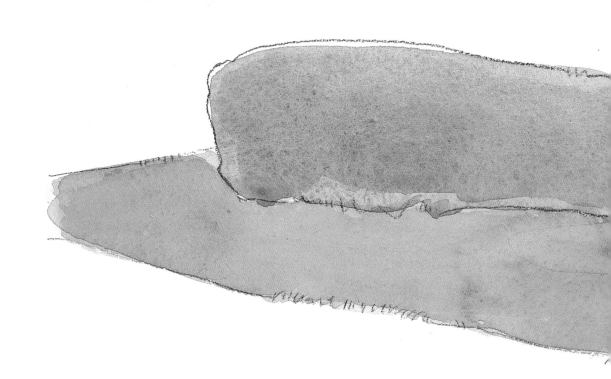

Knock, knock.
No Sam.

No bike.

Tom looks around the house

and under it.

He looks up,

behind, and all around.

No Sam and no bike.

But then . . .

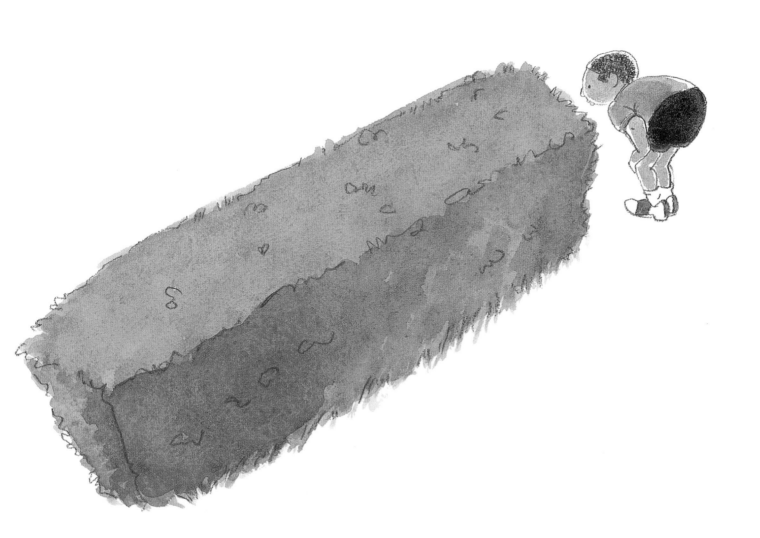

WHIZZZ . . .

Sam rides around in circles,
up and down,

then stops.

"Sorry, Tom."

Tom takes turns with Sam.

They each go up, across,

down, riding away and then back. Until Sam finds . . .

a new bike and helmet.

I Like to Read® books, created by award-winning
picture book artists as well as talented newcomers,
instill confidence and the joy of reading in new readers.

We want to hear every new reader say, "I like to read!"

Visit our website for flash cards, activities, and more about the series:
www.holidayhouse.com/I-Like-to-Read/
#ILTR

This book has been tested by an educational expert
and determined to be a guided reading level F.

To the kids, young and old, who love to ride, especially my daughter Leila

I LIKE TO READ is a registered trademark of Holiday House Publishing, Inc.
Text and illustrations copyright © 2011 by James E. Ransome
All Rights Reserved
HOLIDAY HOUSE is registered in the U.S. Patent and Trademark Office.
The art for this book was created in watercolor with pencil.
Printed and bound in July 2019 at Toppan Leefung, DongGuan City, China.
www.holidayhouse.com
10 9 8 7 6 5 4

Library of Congress Cataloging-in-Publication Data
Ransome, James E.
New red bike! / by James E. Ransome. — 1st ed.
p. cm.
Summary: Tom enjoys the thrill of riding his brand new bicycle, and then shares it with a friend.
ISBN 978-0-8234-2226-5 (hardcover)
[1. Bicycles and bicycling—Fiction. 2. Sharing—Fiction.] I. Title.
PZ7.R1755Ne 2011
[E]—dc22
2010023674

ISBN 978-0-8234-3852-5 (paperback)